THE GREAT FLYTRAP DISASTER

CHRIS MOULD

Hodder
Children's
Books

Hodder Children's Books
An imprint of Hachette Children's Group
Part of Hodder & Stoughton
Carmelite House, 50 Victoria Embankment,
London EC4Y 0DZ
An Hachette UK Company
www.hachette.co.uk

BUTTON

LILY

THE SKIRTING-BOARD MICE

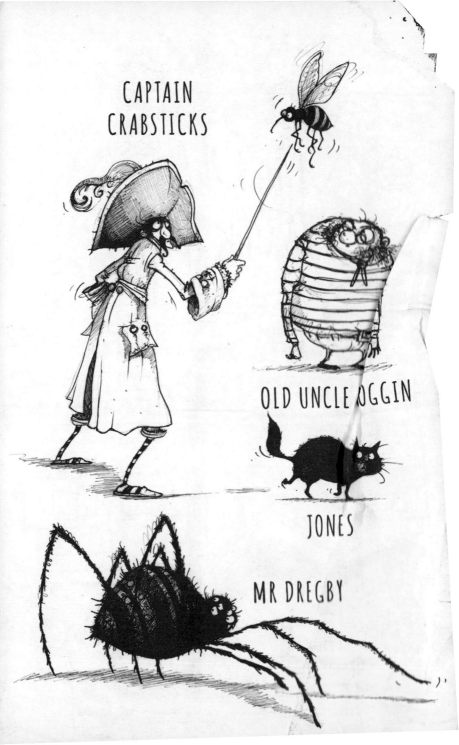

CAPTAIN
CRABSTICKS

OLD UNCLE OGGIN

JONES

MR DREGBY

At the end of the street is an old junk shop. It's gloomy and shabby and nothing ever happens there. At least, that's what most people think ...

Among the odds and ends and things of no use, a dusty ship in a bottle sits gathering cobwebs on a shelf. But when the world isn't watching, a tiny pirate crew comes out to explore.

And when you're smaller than a teacup, a junk shop can be a pretty dangerous place ...

Buzz Bombs

Button awoke to a loud noise. He couldn't quite work out what it was, so he hopped down from his hammock. "What on earth is happening?" he asked, as he climbed through the glass neck of the bottle to see what all the commotion was.

There is no such thing as a normal day on the shelf. When you are smaller than a pepperpot, you are often faced with some kind of wild adventure. And while the Pocket Pirates had been enjoying a good long summer, the blazing sun had brought all sorts of problems. As Captain Crabsticks had just discovered, even a gentle morning's walk past the old books to the candlestick could be filled with deadly terror.

Button was deafened by a terrible buzzing. Rubbing his tired eyes, he caught sight of his captain. Sword drawn, Captain Crabsticks was battling a fly that was as big as a Labrador would be to me and you.

Bzzzzzzzzzzzz it droned, as it darted around him. The Captain thrust

his sword in its direction. The fly was fast, but the sword hand of the Captain was a good match for it.

"Away, you blighter. Go on old chap, shoo." He darted around, darning needle in hand.

Button watched, enjoying the entertainment. "Lily, over here!" he shouted. "I've not seen a good pirate versus insect swordfight for a while." His shipmate and best friend Lily appeared out of the bottle to join him. The flies and wasps had been driving them crazy and hopefully the Captain's steel blade would teach them a lesson.

"How exciting," gasped Lily.

Swoosh. One final swash and buckle

of the sword sent the huge fly swooping across the back of the shelf, but what happened next was not what they'd expected. By now Uncle Noggin had joined them and the crew stood together watching as the fly crashed straight into a huge spiderweb.

"Oh, poor old thing," said the Captain. "I only meant to scare him off."

The crew stood together, looking up at the web. It had always been tucked in the corner, but recently seemed to be growing at an alarming rate. Mr Dregby, the house spider, had been feasting on all the flies which had arrived with the hot weather.

The four Pocket Pirates watched the

poor fly struggle in the sticky silk. Then the spider himself appeared, dancing along the thread to take a look at his prize.

"Well, well, well. Thank you so much, Captain. How VERY kind of you to deliver breakfast. To be perfectly honest I'm still full from my last meal, but I'm sure he'll save for later."

And with that he darted along the thread, back into the corner.

"That spider is getting far too big for his boots," said Button. "And look at the size of that web."

"It's getting closer," grumbled Uncle Noggin. "It'll swallow us all up if we're not careful."

"Don't worry," said Lily. "There's not much chance of him swallowing *you* whole."

"Ooooh, how rude," said Uncle Noggin,

giving her a wink and patting his round belly.

They could still see Mr Dregby's large hairy legs. And when Button looked a little closer, he could spy his six eyes still watching them keenly.

"I think Mr Dregby's grown too," said Lily.

"I wouldn't be surprised," said Uncle Noggin. "His web is like an all-you-can-eat buffet at the moment."

"Well at least it's keeping his belly full," Button pointed out. "I hate it when he looks at me with hungry eyes. It makes me nervous."

Bzzzzzzzzz. Just then another fly swooped by.

"Away, you blustering buzz bomb," cried the Captain, swinging his sword back into action. "That's enough swashbuckling for now. I suggest we all get on board and think about breakfast."

As they returned to the ship, something pattered on the glass bottle above them. Button climbed the mast and perched inside the crow's-nest. It was Mr Dregby, dangling from a strand of web and dropping on to the bottle, his six eyes peering in at them spookily.

"He's never come this close before," Button shouted down to the crew. "I don't like it. We're going to have to deal with him, good and proper."

"Haul in the cork!" ordered the

Captain. The crew
gathered on deck
and Button and
Lily turned the
handle sticking out
of the cotton reel. As
the thread wound its
way in, the cork pulled
into place, blocking the
entrance to the bottle.

"Good work, team. We
don't want unwanted guests at
the table! Now, I seem to think
we have a chunk of boiled egg
and a morsel of sausage to
share out."

"Sounds good," said Button, his

tummy rumbling. "Pirate breakfast is the best meal of the day. Coming right up, Captain."

Too Close for Comfort

"What is the Captain reading?" asked Lily, watching him from her vantage point on the ship's deck. He was lying across the pages of a large book at the back of the shelf. As he read he used his sword to underline the words, mumbling to himself.

"Something about the common

house spider," answered Button, who seemed to be spending most of the day looking out through the telescope from the crow's-nest. "I think it was all that kerfuffle with Mr Dregby. Got him thinking about things eight-legged."

Just then Button spotted Mr Tooey, the junk shop owner. He was walking down the corridor into the main part of the shop, carrying something heavy. Button took hold of the snail shell that was tied to the mast and blew into it, making a loud, horn-like noise. When the crew heard that sound they knew to act quickly. Jones, the ship's cat, yowled as he ran for cover, and

Lily headed inside the ship to
join the Captain and Uncle
Noggin. They couldn't risk
being seen.

Button crouched
low in the crow's-nest,
eyes on Mr Tooey
who was coming
close to the shelf.
Too close.

It always made them nervous when he was near: even the simplest move could change their lives drastically. They lived in fear of a spring clean. One time Mr Tooey had moved everything on to the floor to tidy the shelf, and the skirting-board mice had attacked the ship.

And what was he carrying?

"It's some kind of plant," hissed Button, passing on information to the crew below. "But I've never seen anything like it."

"That's because you don't know anything about plants," said Uncle Noggin. "Here, let me have a look." He edged his head out of the ship so he could see.

Lily rolled her eyes at him. "What is it then, clever clogs?"

"Aha ... eruum, OH, I don't know!" muttered Uncle Noggin. "I ain't never seen anything like it either."

Button kept his eye glued to the spy glass.

Mr Tooey shoved the plant around on the end of the shelf, finding just the right place for it, then he poured a drop of water into the bottom of the pot while his dog fussed around his feet. "There ... that should help," he murmured.

He tottered off into the kitchen, talking to the dog as he went. "Come on then old boy, let's get you something to eat."

"*That should help*?" repeated Button. "What does he mean?"

But no one could answer.

When they were sure he had gone, the Captain gave orders for the cork to be pushed out of the bottle neck and they went outside to look at the curious piece of greenery that had just been delivered.

In the excitement of its arrival, they had forgotten about Mr Dregby.

And now they gazed in wonder at the towering green monster above them. What was it?

"By Jove, I've never seen anything QUITE like that," said the Captain. "Looks like something tropical."

"Might be something we can eat!"
said Uncle Noggin. "Looks like it has
some kind of fruit on it."

Bzzzzzzzz. From the distance,
the droning sound of house flies was
approaching. This time there were
three of them. The Captain drew his
sword and Button grabbed the broken
paintbrush that he used to sweep
the deck.

Bzzzzzzzz. The noise grew louder.

The winged horrors
swooped down at the
buccaneers. Jones
meowed loudly and
Lily climbed up the
candlestick and

waved the pirate
flag at them.
"Shoo, shoo."

Uncle
Noggin rolled
up a corner
of torn
newspaper
and waved
it in the air. "Go
on, off you go. Buzz around somewhere
else, you 'orrible lumps."

"I think they're after our food
supplies," said Button.

"No chance," cried Lily. "We'll fight
to the end!"

Behind them, Mr Dregby had

dropped to the outer edge of his web. He couldn't resist the look of the juicy flies and mini buccaneer snacks.

He dropped again, bouncing towards Button on his strong silky thread.

"Look out behind you!" screamed Lily, but it was too late. Quick as a flash, Mr Dregby wrapped his creepy hairy feelers around Button's head and started doing his best to pull him up into the web.

Lily grabbed hold of Button around the middle, followed swiftly (well when I say swiftly ... errr ... not really) by Old Uncle Noggin, who grabbed on to Lily by the coat tails. So now there was a tug

of war, with Mr Dregby on one side and Button in between, as Lily and Uncle Noggin held tight, refusing to let go.

Captain Crabsticks had finished fighting off the flies. Fearlessly, he climbed on to the top of a cotton reel to wave his darning needle at the huge spider.

"Get those blasted hairy pins of yours away from our cabin boy, you filthy arachnid."

The more the crew pulled at Button, the tighter Mr Dregby's grip became around his neck. He was struggling to breathe and the spiky hairs from the spider's huge legs scratched his face.

Close up, the spider's eyes whizzed

and twirled in every direction and its mouth was opening wide.

"Take that, you … you … eight-legged monkey," the Captain shouted, and at that moment he managed to stick the needle into one of the spider's legs. Mr Dregby made a strange spidery squuueeeeaaaal, let go of Button and went shooting back up his thread into the corner.

"That'll teach him to mess with the might of the miniature pirates!" said the Captain. Retreat to the deck, crew."

Lily and Uncle Noggin dragged Button to his feet and they all hurried inside the bottle. Then, for the second time that day, they pulled the cork tight into the neck. Mr Dregby stared at them, six angry eyes and bared teeth glinting at them through the glass.

"That was too close for comfort," said Lily, her heart beating fast.

"Well done," cheered Old Uncle Noggin. "We deserve a tasty snack for that."

"How long do we have to keep this up for?" said Button, sweating after his ordeal. "It's exhausting."

"And it's red hot today," said Uncle Noggin, wiping his brow with his handkerchief.

The flies bashed against the bottle, buzzing and hovering. Mr Dregby walked over the glass ceiling, wrapping his silk backwards and forwards around the bottle.

"We're being taken over," said Button.

"Something has to be done, and soon," agreed the Captain. "No one and nothing bullies the inch-high pirate crew and gets away with it."

The Crow & The Pitcher

All that heat inside the bottle was making the place feel like a greenhouse. Normally they'd keep their food in the ship, but they'd had to put it in an old matchbox on the shelf to stop it going off. And when Button ventured out to fetch supplies he discovered something.

36

"Garghhhh! The flies have eaten the grub."

"WHAT?" cried Uncle Noggin. "ALL of it?"

"Every last morsel," said Button, hanging his head and pulling his wet hair back over his face. "Except the cheese. They've been sick on the cheese."

"Urrrrrghh, the cheek of it," gasped Uncle Noggin. "I was looking forward to grape juice and cheddar tonight."

"We're stuck in here, it's red hot, I'm bored AND I'm thirsty," said Lily, frowning.

"How about a good old story then?" suggested Uncle Noggin. He *always* had a story, and now was no exception. "It'll help to take our minds off things."

"A story? What ... now? Why?" said Lily, folding her arms and still looking cross. She settled into her hammock as Old Uncle Noggin perched on a timber of the ship that stuck out at an angle.

"Go on," said Button, sitting down

alongside them. "It will take our minds off the mayhem."

"Well, you reminded me, being thirsty an' all that, about the story of a clever old crow. It's an ancient story, mind you. But it's a good 'un."

"OK," said Lily, "I'm all ears."

"Well, it was a hot afternoon in the middle of a blisterin' summer when a crow swooped down to see if he could find water to drink. There didn't seem to be a drop *anywhere*. Not until he found a shady corner of a garden and an old jug that had collected rainwater from a thick nest of old vine leaves.

"But the jug was only half full and try as he might, the crow just couldn't

reach far enough to take a drink. Not even with his long beak."

"What did he do, what did he do?" urged Button.

"Well, he took hold of a pebble in his beak and dropped it into the water."

"Why?" asked Button.

"*Listen*," said Lily, "and you'll find out."

"Then another and another, until slowly he could see that the water was beginning to rise upwards.

"He kept on going, one pebble after another. Hard work it was too, for an old crow. Backwards and forwards in the heat and starting to feel like it wasn't worth it after a while.

"But when eventually the water came to the top, he took a good long drink and then flew off up into the blue sky, feeling happy and satisfied."

"Ahh, that's clever," said Button.

"Of course," said Uncle Noggin. "Mr Crow's a wise old stick."

"That was very good, Uncle Noggin. Thank you. But it hasn't helped our situation. AND it's made me more thirsty," said Lily.

But Button thought he might know what the story really meant. They had to be wise, just like the crow.

First things first. They would need a late-night trip to try to get some supplies. A good climb in the dark down to the old desk, where they knew there was dried pasta in the drawer with the broken keyhole.

Pasta was light and easy to carry. Then they'd draw off some hot water from the leaky pipe and soak it until it went soft. Not the best meal, but at least it stopped them feeling hungry.

Button pattered over to the wristwatch that was fastened to the wall. It was late. Mr Tooey would be snoring away upstairs by now and more importantly, the dog would be fast asleep. It was a good time to leave. He was looking forward to it: a short breathing space, away from the shelf. A bit of adventure, maybe a touch of danger. Or at least some peace and quiet away from Uncle Noggin.

"I think you're right," said Lily. "Let's take our time. As long as we keep an eye out for Old Hairy Legs, it should be fun."

When darkness came, Button and Lily

set off together, leaving the Captain and Uncle Noggin to look after the ship.

It was cooler now the light had dropped. A silvery-blue moon lit the way, and for a moment it felt almost magical along the shelf.

As they skirted around the plant pot, something made a sound.

"What was that?" hissed Button.

"What?" whispered Lily.

"It was a … strange sound. Like a shhquelch but not just a shhhquelch. More like a thump but not just a thump. Kind of both. A kind of …"

"You mean a *shhhhquelllllump*?" said Lily.

"Yes, *exactly*," said Button. "You

heard it too, right? What was it?"

"No, I didn't hear it. No idea!"
said Lily. They carried on and the
shhhhquellllump was soon forgotten.

Climbing down to the desk was an
easy task for Lily and Button, especially
when they were alone. In no time at all
they were rooting around in the drawer
with the broken keyhole.

"This one will do," said Button, after
they had spent some time searching
through the rubble. He was brushing
down a piece of macaroni. They had
no idea why the dried pasta sat among
the paper clips and staples, but it was
useful. Lily found one too, and with
an old shoelace and a safety pin they

started hauling their meal back to the
shelf.

Climbing over the odds and ends,
Button noticed a book on plants. He
couldn't resist investigating the
pages in the blue moonlight.

"What are you doing?"
Lily whispered back
to him.

"I just thought ...
I might ..." (every
time he found

a picture or an interesting paragraph he
went silent, studied it and carried on
again) "... be able to see ..."

"Be able to see *what*?"

"AHA ... there it is!" he said,
stopping at a picture of a plant that
looked identical to the one Mr Tooey
had brought to the shelf.

"Oh ..." said Button, "Look ... it's a
V E N U S   F L Y T R A P."

"What's a veenos flytrap?"

"V E N U S," said Button. "It's ...
oh my goodness, it says here it's
carnivorous! Catches its prey in a trap,
triggered by tiny hairs."

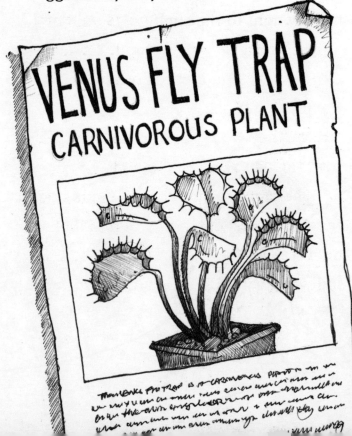

Button heaved hard on the book's cover with both hands and slammed it shut. "Lily, we need to warn the Captain and Uncle Noggin."

"Why? What does 'car ... ni ... vorous' mean?"

"It means it eats living creatures," said Button, "If that thing gets hold of any of us, we'll be plant food. We need to be quick ... and let the others know. Come on, let's get going."

Off they went, making slow progress over the messy odds and ends.

The moon went behind a cloud and they stumbled in the dim light. Lily held on to the back of Button's waistcoat, following carefully, but suddenly it was

gone. He wasn't there!

She stopped still and called out. "Button, where did you go? ... Button?"

"Here," came his voice in the dark. "I think I'm trapped."

"Where?"

"Don't come near," he insisted. "It's ... I think it's ..."

"What?"

"It's silky and sticky. I think ... I'm stuck in the web."

"NO," said Lily, panicking. "I'll get you out!" But she slipped and within a moment she'd fallen inside the deep well of a milk jug, grazing her knees and banging her elbows and head.

Mr Dregby pattered towards them

through the darkness. He came up close to Button, his six eyes looking him up and down.

"Well, well, well ... how exciting!" He circled Button, wrapping him up in silky thread. "One served up on a plate ... and one in the cupboard for later," he chuckled, peering into the jug. "What a fine menu. I shall look forward to feeling hungry again. For the moment I shall return to my corner and sleep off my last meal. Don't go away now. I shall look forward to having you for dinner tomorrow. Goodnight, children. Sleep well."

The Rescuers

"Hmmmm. I wonder why those shoddy shipmates still haven't got back," said the Captain. "I'm presuming they haven't been squished or eaten."

"Perhaps we should go and check," suggested Uncle Noggin. "You never know what's around at this time of night."

"Well, I guess a stroll along the shelf won't hurt. Let's see what we can see, shall we?"

Uncle Noggin got himself up out of his favourite piece of sponge, and Captain Crabsticks sprang on to his feet. Jones lifted his head, meowed and went back to sleep.

"That's right old chap, you keep an eye on the camp," said the Captain. "We won't be long. Back in a whisker." He stroked Jones' head and tickled his chin, making him purr loudly.

Only Button's face could be seen sticking out from the coiled-up silky sleeping bag that he was now trapped in. He couldn't see Lily in the bottom of the jug and she couldn't see him stuck in the webbing. But they could hear each other.

"Try not to shout out or move," said Lily. "You'll vibrate the web and it'll bring Mr Dregby back down. We should try to escape while he sleeps."

"Good thinking," said Button. "But how?"

"I'm not sure yet. I'm thinking."

"Me too."

The silhouettes of Uncle Noggin and the Captain wandered along in the darkness. A quick stroll along the shelf had revealed nothing. It was still and silent. Something wasn't right.

"I say, old Noggin, how about we climb up on to that greenery and take a look out from the top there?" suggested the Captain.

Uncle Noggin was none too keen on climbing. "Oh I don't know, Cap'n, my back isn't what it used to be you know and ..." but before he could protest any further he was already lagging behind.

Button heard the voices coming closer. The familiar sound of his captain for sure, and the puffing and panting and complaining of Uncle Noggin.

"Come on old chap, keep up," said

the Captain, climbing the side of the pot like a monkey.

Lily could hear them too. She had to make them hear her, even from inside the jug. She bellowed a loud "*HELP!*" and it echoed around her.

"Well, shiver me seashells," said the Captain. "I think I can hear a cry for help."

"Can't hear nothing!" replied Uncle Noggin, who was now pulling himself up on to a huge spiky green flower. "Let me climb a bit higher."

"HEEEEELP!"

"Ah, there it goes. It's young Lily. Don't worry, we'll be there in no time, old girl," called the Captain. "Where the devil are you?"

"Milk jug!"

"Don't go near the plant," said
Button, but he couldn't shout because he
knew he'd vibrate the web.

"Can't hear you, old chap. Be there in
a minute. Just as soon I've reached the
top of this plant."

"Arghhh NOOOO!" shouted Lily, but
by now her crewmates were climbing
over the green tendrils and standing
on the flower heads. "Get away from
it, it's—"

"Ah there you are, Button old chap.
Fear not, we'll have you out of there in
no ti—" *SHHHHQUELLLLUMP!*

"Well that's strange," said Old
Uncle Noggin, "one minute the

Captain was right there in front of
me and the next minute he was g—"
SHHHHQUELLLLUMP!

Suddenly it was silent. The sounds
of Uncle Noggin and Captain Crabsticks
rambling on and tugging themselves
along to make a rescue had stopped
completely.

"Oh dear," squeaked Button quietly
from his cocoon. "Lily, I know where
the *shhhhquellllump* came from."

"Where?"

"From the flytrap. When it ... you
know ... *catches* ... something."

As Button spoke, he spotted the
Captain and Uncle Noggin, who had
just managed to poke their heads out

from the spiky pods that had clamped
down on them.

"Ahh, I see," said the Captain, "the
venus flytrap. Yes of course, I knew I

recognised it. Now ... errr, let me see. Don't worry, old chap, I'll have us out of here before you can say Davy Jones' Locker."

Uncle Noggin's trap struggled to close around his rounded shape, but it was pulling so tight at him he couldn't move.

Button's face stuck out of his silk sleeping bag. Lily sat helpless in the bottom of the jug. And the two old sea dogs lay wrapped up in their spiky coats with their heads peeping out at the top.

"What now, Captain?" said Button. "Any ideas?"

"Errrum ... bear with me, old chap ...

I'm thinking."

They waited in darkness and silence and not one of them could imagine what they should do next.

Mr Dregby opened his eyes. His prize was still waiting. *Not long before breakfast*, he smiled. And then he went back to sleep.

Captain Jones

The night moved on. Outside the shop window the stars shone and an owl hooted in the distance. Everyone lay trapped in their junk-shop prisons, growing tired but knowing that time was not on their side. If they went to sleep it would be disastrous. They might not ever wake up again!

The Captain and Uncle Noggin tried hard to wriggle free. They pushed and pulled with their arms and legs, but it seemed that the more they struggled inside the spiky pods, the tighter they closed around them.

"Best keep as still as possible, old Noggin. Looks like we're in for a tricky evening."

For a moment Lily thought she had a solution. "If I can rock the bottom of the milk jug, I can tip it right over and climb out," she said, explaining her plan to Button as she began to put her brainwave into action. It was a simple idea but it could work. If she could break free she could cut the others down from their traps. She ran from side to side, banging her hands on the rounded walls at each end until she felt the base lifting slightly from the floor. The jug gradually began to rock on its base until it was swaying.

"Keep going!" said Button. "It's working, it's moving. If you get out of there you can free us all!" He was beginning to shout loudly in excitement. The spider stirred in his sleep.

The jug rocked from side to side, the movements getting bigger until eventually ... CRASH. It overbalanced, and with it went a stack of bits and pieces that had been piled up next to it. Matchboxes and pepper pots. Paper clips and drawing pins. Some dice, a pine cone, and a pile of old coins spilled across the shelf, and a cotton reel went rolling off the edge.

The jug had tipped over, but not all the way. The mustard-pot bath tub had stopped it. Lily still couldn't climb out.

"Ah, drat," said Lily, puffing and panting, "I'm worn out." She sat to catch her breath. "All that effort for nothing."

"Do you mind?" said Old Uncle Noggin. "I'm trying to die in peace."

Just then a strange tunnel of light appeared in the room. It was Mr Tooey. He had heard the noise and came peering over at them with a torch. The glare was blinding and they stayed still, panic-stricken as the searchlight seemed to peer right into their faces.

"More pests," he muttered. "Where are you?" And he ran the torch along the shelf.

And then suddenly he was gone and all that could be heard was, "If I ever get

hold of those mangy mice I'll feed them to the alley cats."

"Phew, it's OK. He's gone. Good try, Lily," whispered Button. "I've been thinking. Maybe if I can stretch this web far enough, I can tear it away from the wall." He pressed his feet against the plaster and began to push. He kept going until he was on the tips of his toes.

The web stretched around him. He felt the silk straining and he could hear bits of thread springing and snapping. It took all his strength. He could feel his legs growing weak but he kept on pushing. He was almost there.

But the web was too strong and

when it had gone as far as it would go it sprang back and flattened him against the wall with a thud, keeping a tight hold on him.

Eight legs pattered down the silk and six narrowed eyes glared at him. "Now, now, Button. You're testing my patience. All your fidgeting is keeping me awake."

Mr Dregby pulled a length of Button's emergency shoelace from his backpack and with his pincers he shredded it to pieces. Button watched the sharp jaws effortlessly cut into the rope.

"The more you annoy me, the crosser I get. Do you understand, Button?"

Then Mr Dregby wrapped him up

tighter with his silvery string and returned to his corner.

Button gulped and felt his heart thumping hard in his chest. A bead of sweat ran down his forehead.

"You know how long a spider ACTUALLY keeps its victims in its web, don't you, Button?" said Uncle Noggin.

"Yes, I do, and I don't wish to remind myself, thank you."

"Just thought it might inspire you to escape," shrugged the old pirate.

"Sure," Button answered. "Want to know how a venus flytrap eats its prey? Holds on to it tight and slowly digests every inch of it by releasing a nasty chemical and dissolving its victim."

"Oh ... well, yes I knew that, Button. Thank you. In fact I think I can feel it happening right now."

"There'll be nothing left of us," cried Lily from the milk jug. "You'll be plant food and me and Button will be spider breakfast. The Pocket Pirates will be extinct."

"Nonsense," said the Captain, "I'll have us out of here in no time."

He looked around, racking his brain, and realising there wasn't much he could do with his body gripped tight from the head downwards.

"Errrum ... but if I don't," he continued, "then I've had a thought ..."

"What is it?" said Button.

"Well, we can't leave the ship without a captain. Someone needs to look after her."

"And ...?"

"So, if we're no longer here ... I hereby declare Jones will be captain of the ship ... just in case!"

"Pah, charming," laughed Button.

"I'm trapped in the web of a giant spider. There's no real hope of escaping and I'm likely to be breakfast in only a matter of hours. And if by any miracle I manage to escape, my Captain is going to be a soggy old grey moggy."

No one answered. Button was exhausted. They *all* were. It had been a long day. Button felt himself drifting, his eyes closing. The silk cocoon, fastened tight around his body, was somehow comfortable. He tried to fight the urge, but he was helpless and eventually he drifted off into sleep.

An Unexpected Meal

BZzzzzZZZzzzzzZZZzzzzzzz.

The very thing that had woken
Button the previous morning suddenly
roused him again. But this time he
was glad of it. He turned his head,
his eyes staring into darkness. He felt
a tightness around him and quickly
remembered that the comfortable feel

of his hammock had been replaced with silky spider thread and that he was in great danger.

"Wake up," said Button, whispering carefully over to the Captain. But it was no good. The Captain couldn't hear him, and Button dared not wake the terrible Mr Dregby by shouting too loud.

Fortunately for the Captain, the fly buzzed over to him and landed on his face, shocking him into opening his eyes. His cry of surprise woke Uncle Noggin, who until now had been dribbling over the side of the spiky plant.

Old Noggin went into a sudden panic. "I can't feel my legs!

Arrrgghhhhhhh! It's eaten half of me
already!"

"Shhhhhhhhh," said Lily from the
milk jug.

"Calm down, you old walrus.
You're all there, I can see from
here. I've been dreaming about
spiders," said the Captain.

81

"Must have been that book I was reading. Interesting creature, the common house spider, he's a recycler ... a bit like us I suppose. Eats his web so that he can spin one again if he doesn't get too much food in the meantime."

"Clever idea. Isn't nature amazing! Not much of a meal though," said Uncle Noggin, distracted by the talk of food.

"Oh, I don't know! Tastier than Button, I expect," said the Captain, chuckling.

"Oh, very funny," huffed Button. "This is no time for jokes. We need to think fast."

"I'm trying," said the Captain.

"No you're not, you're half asleep."

And then Button had a thought. "What was that bit again?" he asked. "The bit about eating its web."

"Well, apparently the web is made from protein, so instead of wasting it, he can gobble it up it and then produce more spider silk."

"Ah, I see. You mean a bit like packing up your tent and moving on to another campsite," came a voice from the jug.

"Very good, old chap," said the Captain. "Exactly like that."

Button didn't say anything else. He didn't need to. He took a glance above him to check that Mr Dregby was still asleep. In the distance he could see some hairy legs sticking out from the web. They were still.

It was early, but a faint light was starting to come through the window. This will work, he said to himself. I know it will.

He began to tear at the web with his teeth. After all, they were the only thing he could use. But it was obvious: he would eat his way out, just like the spider eats his web.

Button was tearing out great chunks, but it wasn't pleasant. It stuck to his face like candy floss, and tasted like a mouthful of belly button fluff. He spat it out below, and soon he had freed the tight coil around his neck. Leaning over

towards his shoulders, he chewed away
until they were free too.

He went slowly, so that the web
didn't vibrate, but it didn't take long
before he was easing his body out at
the top, freeing his hands. Then he was

pulling and tearing at the thread around his legs, and he knew that he was almost ready to make the leap.

Stretching his fingertips as far as he could, he reached the edge of the nearby mirror frame, and pulling himself towards it, felt his feet come out of his shoes, leaving them behind. He was free!

The Captain and Uncle Noggin had been watching Button's every move. They kept still and silent. If they made a fuss now the old eight-legged beast

would appear and
it would all go
wrong again. They
waited and watched
in wonder at the
antics of the lad
who they knew was
the best cabin boy in
the world.

Button climbed
across the mirror
frame, using his hands
and feet to hang on,
and when he had gone
as far as he needed
he dropped on to
the shelf.

"Right," he said, rubbing his hands. "Time for the tiniest of the mini pirate crew to show how brave he really is."

Button Bites Back

Button went over to the plant pot and stood beneath the venus flytrap.

"Don't worry," he called. "I'll have you chaps out of there in no time. But Lily comes first. If that eight-legged beast wakes up and decides he's hungry, he'll see I'm gone and drop straight into the jug for his breakfast."

"But what if we get eaten by the plant?" said Uncle Noggin.

"Don't worry, it takes days," Button reassured him. "Did I not mention that? I read it in a book."

"But what if Dregby decides he likes the look of US? We're trapped and helpless."

"He won't come anywhere near this plant," said the Captain bravely. "These things don't just eat flies, they eat anything. Spiders, bugs … oh, and small pirates of course."

"What are you going to do, Button?" asked Uncle Noggin.

"You'll see," whispered Button. He ran to perch on a pile of old books, level with the top of the milk jug. Lily's familiar face was staring up at him out of the dark.

"Have you out of there in no time, old girl," said Button, pulling his emergency rope from his backpack. And then he was reminded that now it had been shredded it was nowhere near as long as it needed to be.

"Ah, drat. Suffering seashells," said Button. "Now what do I do?" He knew he needed to be extra careful not to fall in that jug or they'd both be a free meal and that would be the end of everybody.

Whatever his alternative plan was, it needed to be foolproof. He looked around, but couldn't see anything that

would work. There was a pencil, but it wasn't long enough. There had been a cotton reel, but Button had watched it roll off the shelf when the jug crashed into the corner. And the other reels lying around were empty – the thread had already been used for various adventures.

He stood on the books, scratched his chin and leaned against the water pipe.

And then, in a moment, it came to him. "Of course!" he whispered, a smile breaking across his face.

"What is it?" said Lily, "*What?* What do you mean, '*Of course!*'?"

"The story, Lily, you know. The crow and the jug."

"I need more of a clue than that!"

"You'll need to swim," said Button, pointing to the water pipe. "Look, this is where we take the cork out to fill the bath," he said, pointing to where the little bung had been forced into the leak so that when they wanted to take a bath in the mustard pot, they could fill it with water.

The jug had crashed into the corner and was in just the right position. Button pulled on the cork and the lukewarm water started dribbling out.

"It's a bit like your story," Button pointed out to Old Uncle Noggin, "except the other way round. I'm pouring water into the jug until Lily rises to the top!

Then when she's out, we'll get you both down."

"You're a clever old stick, aren't you, Button," said the Captain proudly.

"My feet are getting wet," said Lily. The water was filling her boots and there was nothing she could do but stand in it and wait for it to rise.

The jug was filling nicely, but the light from the window was growing brighter. Dawn was on the way.

"Keep going, you're doing a marvellous job," said the Captain.

"Yes ... hurry up!" said Uncle Noggin. "I think my feet are being eaten alive."

"Uncle Noggin, even the grubbiest plant on earth wouldn't be interested in your feet," laughed Button.

"Don't worry, you're safe," called Lily from below as the water reached her neck.

The water was swirling around her now. She had to keep kicking her feet to stay upright and she could feel herself starting to float up inside the jug.

"It's working, Button. It's working!"

But up above in the corner, something could hear Lily's voice. It opened its eyes. There were six of them.

At first Mr Dregby was sleepy. But then he remembered, and he was excited about his breakfast.

He came out of his hole, stretching his legs and bouncing along his thread towards the place where Button had been. But when he got there the bundle was empty, torn to shreds. What in the world had happened to the juicy young prize he had captured? Nothing had ever escaped from his web before.

Mr Dregby's eyes turned red. He grumbled and grimaced with his sharp

teeth. His prickly hairs stood on end.
Off he went to search: surely Button
wasn't far away. But there were so
many crevices and hiding places to
be checked.

Button had climbed back to the
shelf, to think about how to rescue
his other shipmates as soon as Lily
was free.

"I'm almost there!" called Lily. But as
she reached for the edge of the jug, the
eyes that were looming back at her did
not belong to Button. And there were six
of them.

A Brush With The Enemy

Captain Crabsticks had drifted off to
sleep again, wrapped in his spiky green
sleeping bag. Uncle Noggin was awake,
worrying about being eaten alive, trying
to distract himself with thoughts of
food. At that moment he was imagining
a crisp, full-size cornflake.

If Button had looked he would

have seen Uncle Noggin chewing an imaginary mouthful, but he was too busy studying the escape plan to take any notice of Uncle Noggin's nonsense.

He climbed the books again, hoping that Lily would be floating high enough to be pulled out, but when he got there something was in the way. He couldn't quite make it out at first: a dark shape looming over the edge of the jug.

"Dregby!"

Lily was gasping and panicking in the water. She flapped her arms and kicked her legs. Above her, hairy legs hung down. Large teeth were frighteningly close to her face.

"Well well well," said the spider. "What good news. I *will* be getting my breakfast after all."

He dropped a little lower. Close up, his eyes were even meaner.

But just as she let out a yelp, a huge splash soaked Mr Dregby. Button had

pushed a pepper pot into the water! The
spider flew back up his thread in shock,

so sopping wet he looked ridiculous.

Button's face appeared over the side of the jug, grinning a wide grin. He leaned into the jug as far as he could. "Give me your hands, Lil. I can reach you from here."

Lily reached up. Their fingers were almost touching. "Just a little bit further," she gasped.

Button stretched down further. If he wasn't careful he'd be in the water too! With a strong kick, Lily grabbed his hands ... and somehow, between them, they managed to ease her over the rim of the jug and out on to the pile of books.

Mr Dregby was as angry as he was

soaking wet. His breakfast, lunch and dinner plans had been foiled.

"Those pesky miniature pirates have escaped my clutches once again," he moaned as he dried his hairy legs. "Flies for breakfast. I've had enough of those little buzzballs to last me a lifetime. And their noise is keeping me awake at night."

Lily and Button tumbled quickly down the books and up to the shelf. All the commotion had woken Captain Crabsticks again, and Uncle Noggin had been distracted from his dream about cornflakes.

"I'm drenched!" said Lily. "But glad to be alive, thanks to you." She perched on a rusty teaspoon, shivering.

　　Button scratched his head and looked at the flytrap.

"Get me first," said Uncle Noggin. "I can't feel my body. I think there's only my head left."

"I doubt if it could have eaten that much, old chap," said the Captain from his perch.

Lily was looking around for something they might use to prise open the jaws of the hungry green monster. There it was! In the corner, covered in dust and stringy broken bits of cobweb. An old cocktail stick.

She darted over to it and leaned it against the wall, stamping on it until it snapped in half.

"This is perfect," Button said, as she handed one half of it to him.

Just then Mr Dregby dropped down right in front of his face. His eyes were all agog, his teeth were showing. He was still dripping with water.

"Just tell me, Button. How did you get out of my trap? That's all I want to know."

"Stay away from me, Dregby," said Button, pointing the stick at him.

"Oh dear … you're shaking, Button. I thought you were a fearless pirate! Perhaps you're not so brave after all."

"Come any closer and you'll be on the end of this cocktail stick." Button gripped it harder and stood his ground.

"I haven't done with you yet, Button. Don't get too clever. You're only a weedy cabin boy."

And then Mr Dregby crawled back into his dark corner, while Button tried to stop his knees from trembling.

"Thank you, Button," said Lily, who was shaking with cold and a little bit of fright. "You're a hero."

Special Delivery

Button climbed on to Lily's shoulders,
hoisting himself up into the bottom
of the plant pot. As he landed in the
soil, he realised he was still without
his shoes. He took a look up at the web
and could still see the buckles showing
through the thread. How would he ever
get them back?

"First things first," he said to himself. Maybe later, when they'd rescued the rest of the pirate crew.

"You're too late," cried Uncle Noggin. "There's barely anything left of me."

"Don't be silly," said Lily. "Calm yourself down. We'll have you out of there in a flash."

Button decided

that he would get Uncle Noggin out first, because he couldn't bear listening to the moaning any more. He climbed carefully up to the old pirate's pod, making sure he didn't get near any more of the hungry green spiky mouths.

Reaching Uncle Noggin, he shoved one end of the cocktail stick inside the green pod and then he heaved it back with all his might, easing Uncle Noggin out bit by bit. As soon as he could move, Uncle Noggin couldn't get out fast enough. And when he did he yelled out loud.

"I'm alive!" he shouted. "I'm alive! Look, I'm all here! Arms, legs, hands and feet. Little bit achey, mind you. Little bit

sore. These bones aren't
getting any younger, you
know, Button."

Lily helped Old
Noggin down from the
pot and then nipped up
the plant herself.

"Well done, old chap.
Now if you don't mind, I
wouldn't mind getting out
of here myself," pointed out
the Captain. And so, with
Lily's help, Button pulled
him out from the deadly pod.

"You're a bit gooey!" said
Button. "You'll probably need
a bath."

Both the Captain and Uncle Noggin were covered in a sticky, slimy, green mess, and there was a slightly odd smell coming from them.

"Well, at least it will put the flies off," laughed Lily as she climbed back down, avoiding the pods.

At last, they all gathered on the shelf. The older ones covered in green goo, Lily soaking wet and frozen, and Button without his shoes. None of them had managed a night's sleep, and they were still extremely hungry.

Jones came running up to them and brushed against Button's legs.

"Ah there you are Jones, old boy. Well done for playing captain while we were trapped. You did a marvellous job. Extra fish for you tonight."

"So much has happened I can't remember what we were trying to do before all this started," sighed Lily.

"Well, we're trying to fight off the flies, and they'd taken all our food, and old Dregby was getting far too close ..." said Button.

"Ah, that's right," said the Captain. "Now—"

Just then the Captain was interrupted by a delivery. Something bundled in thread came dangling by a single strand of silk above their heads. Slowly it came down until it was in midair in front of Button's face.

121

They looked up to see Dregby on
the ceiling, lowering the parcel like
some kind of spooky, eight-legged
postman.

"Special delivery for your cabin boy,
Captain."

Button took the parcel in his hands.
It was his shoes! He could see the gold
buckles through the silvery thread. He
tried to tear the webbing open but it
was wrapped too tightly so he bit into
it, tearing with his teeth.

The shoes were in there all right, just as he'd left them. It wasn't a trick.

"Why did you do that?" called Button, looking up at the spider.

"Why did I do *what*?" came the voice from above.

"Give me my shoes back? Why would you do that?"

"I wanted to see how you got out of my trap," said Mr Dregby. "And now that I know you used your teeth, next time I'll wrap that mouth shut so you can't bite your way out. I'll get you in the end, Button."

And then he was gone again, through his silvery silk doorway and into his corner.

"Don't worry, Button, he won't ever get you. Not a chance," said Lily.

Button was cross. "Hmmm, we never got a chance to deal with that web, did we?" he muttered to himself. "I've got a plan. I need a shoelace from the sea chest, and a cotton reel. A darning needle and some grease. I'll show that spider not to mess with the Pocket Pirates."

Perfect Plans & Sausages

No one knew quite what Button had in mind, but they went along with it because when Button had a plan, it usually worked a treat. The shipmates watched him hook up the cotton reel to the shoelace and hold it in place with the darning needle. Then he fastened it to the old music box.

And only when they saw him haul the
shoelace around the plant pot did they
see what he was doing. He smeared the
grease along the shelf from the plant pot
towards the corner.

"Uncle Noggin, I want you to use your strength to wind the lever as far as it will go on the music box."

"Aye aye, cabin boy," nodded Uncle Noggin. He hobbled along the shelf to the music box, and he and the Captain leaned against it as he turned the lever until it was fully wound. The music started to play, the barrel turned and pulled the shoelace until, in turn, it pulled the plant pot along the shelf. Lily and Button helped it along with a good old shove from behind and, gliding over the grease, it sailed smoothly into place under Dregby's web.

"Jolly good work, Button old boy," said the Captain.

Outside the bottle, Mr Tooey was wandering around with a sausage sandwich in his hand when something distracted him. He put his sandwich down and stared hard. Had he really put that plant pot there? He could have sworn he'd placed it further over, in the sunlight. Oh well, never mind. He picked up the little watering can from the shop window and soaked the plant through. Then, distracted by something else, he wandered off again.

When the Pocket Pirates ventured out again, Mr Dregby had retreated right back into the corner.

"Your plan worked a treat, Button," said Lily. "Well done."

"Good work," said Uncle Noggin. "He's packed up his tent and moved along."

"Now listen here. Open your ears, buccaneers. Did someone order a takeaway?" said the Captain.

"Not much chance of that!" groaned Lily.

"Stop teasing," said Uncle Noggin. "I'm considering eating some dusty old cobweb at the moment."

"If I don't eat soon, I'll be ill," said Button.

"Well, there's a huge sandwich at the end of the shelf, so if I were you I'd get moving. Tally ho!" shouted the Captain. "Let's get what we can!"

Was it true? Was there really a sandwich at the end of the shelf? Perhaps it was an illusion, brought on by lack of food.

"Oh my goodness," whispered Button. "I think it's ... sausage."

"SAUSAGE!" yelled the crew. "ATTACKKKKK!"

The pirate crew raced towards the gigantic meat feast. Together they moved like a well-oiled machine,

removing the huge lengths of meat,
scooping up the butter, pulling off
chunks of bread and munching as they
went along.

There was nothing like the surprise
of food being delivered to the door. It
hadn't happened often but Mr Tooey

couldn't have chosen a better time.

They retreated below deck and ate and drank until they were almost bursting.

All was good. Mr Dregby was back in his corner and now their bellies were full. And they were so exhausted that in a short while they were all snoring in their hammocks.

"Now where did I put that sandwich? Oh, of course, on the shelf when I watered the plant," muttered Mr Tooey.

He was sure of it. But when he returned to the main part of the shop, he couldn't believe his eyes. Where his sandwich had been were just a few crusts, and what looked like tiny footprints in a smudge of ketchup.

"Not again. I must be dreaming," he groaned.

But of course he would never say anything about it. People would think him mad. Wouldn't they?

Doyle's basket

BACK DOOR   HALLWAY

REAR → HALLWAY

STORE ROOM →

SITTING ROOM →

HALL

Mice

BOOK SHELF

**Don't miss
Button and Lily's
next swashbuckling adventure!**

THE GREAT TREASURE HUNT

CHRIS MOULD

COMING
SOON